Pans

Pans

Riley

snap

apan

napa

Riley

animal gambill

Riley's Bow-Wow Blast

Illustrated by T. B. Jackson-Williams

Boss Paws Publishing, LLC

Written For My Nephew, Nathan
And
Dedicated To Jitterbug
(My "Tiny Tiger" of 15 Years)
- a.g.

Thanks a Bow-Wow Bunch:

Dan Colon

Dave Armstrong

Bill Butler

Jill Keeney

My Furry Children

My Family and Friends

The Animal Community

Riley's Bow-Wow Blast

Text copyright © 2005 by Animal Gambill

Illustrations copyright © 2005 by Animal Gambill

All rights reserved. Boss Paws Publishing, LLC. Associated logos are
trademarks and / or registered trademarks of Animal Gambill.

ISBN 0-9769058-0-9

Printed in China

Creative Direction and Book Design by Dan Colon

Hi. My name is Riley... and I have a "FURRIFIC" story to tell you about my new mom. She is only 8 years old, but she came up with the coolest plan to help me deal with a big problem that I don't usually talk about.

Turn the page and see how my big problem was turned into a Bow-Wow Blast!

I knew my mom was special the first time I saw her at the animal
rescue shelter. I was lying in my dog kennel hoping to be adopted
when she came cruising through the door.
She sang: "I love puppy dogs... I'm here to say... It's time to
sing and dance and play... I'm getting jiggy with my feet...
So rock your paws to the bow-wow beat!"

I perked up right away. I saw a little girl with red curls, light-brown freckles, and a big, bright smile. She had the happiest voice I ever heard.

I was so excited that my tail almost wagged itself into the next room. Before I knew it, I was playing with the little girl and her parents.

Forever Home

They will rub my belly

They will give me baths

They will feed me

They will love me

They will play with me

They will take me to the vet

RILEY

The rescue worker asked the girl's parents if they could give me a safe and loving "Forever Home" which means I never leave them. I liked the sound of that!

Everything was going really well.
Then it happened....... The rescue
worker told the little girl and her parents
my secret. The worker said, "Riley is a great dog and he loves
kids, but he gets very scared during thunderstorms. He shakes,
he whines, and he pants. Sometimes, he even tries to run away."

Oh no... my secret was out.
I knew it was important for them to know I needed special care,
but what if they didn't want me now?
I started to think they may not be the right family for me.
That is when I heard the little girl begin to sing...

Don't be scared, Riley... I have a plan...
I will help you feel safe as best I can.
What do you say, Mom? What do you say, Dad?
We must help Riley so he won't be sad.

The little girl's parents looked at each other and smiled.
"Okay, Singin' Sally," her father said, "Let's take Riley home."
I couldn't believe it! I was going to have a new home!
I was also going to have a new mom named Singin' Sally!

With a name like Singin' Sally, she had to be cool
But I wondered about her "plan." How could a little girl
help me feel safe during a big storm?

That afternoon, I explored my new yard.
When I finished checking out all the different smells, Singin' Sally
led me to the back door of the house. She smiled and said, "Riley, it's time for
the Puppy Dog Power Plan. As part of the plan, you get to meet a new friend. He
has four legs like you, and he loves to chase tennis balls. His name is Lordy."
Singin' Sally then opened the door and a big, black dog bounced over to me.

He dropped a thick toy rope at my feet.
I picked it up. He grabbed the other end
and we started to play tug-of-war.

Hi, I'm Hobo Kitty. I live with
Singin' Sally too. She's cool... but
these dogs are critter crazy.

A little later, Singin' Sally showed us how to play
a game called "hide-n-seek."

I liked this new game. Lordy liked it too, but he's not very good at hiding. Singin' Sally said we need to play like this when it storms. She said we need to stay busy having fun. This is all part of the Puppy Dog Power Plan.

Two days later, we got to test the first part of the plan.
Lordy and I had just finished playing a game of chase.
I was turbo tired. Soon, I was falling asleep and starting
to dream about one of my favorite things to do...

...go for a "Riley Ride" in the car.

I dreamed that the wind was blowing my whiskers and wiggling my
gold, wavy fur. I was sportin' my sunglasses and jammin' to some
cool music on the radio. I was having a Bow-Wow Blast!

Then, out of nowhere,
I heard a very loud KABOOM-CRACKLE-KABOOM!
My dream ended and I opened my eyes. I jumped up and looked out
the window. The sky turned black. I saw a big Zig-Zag flash of light.
The rain was dropping out of the clouds in buckets. My heart went
thump - thump... thump - thump... faster and faster. I was scared!

I wanted to run away from the storm, so I looked for some way
to get out of the house. Suddenly, the wind blew the door open.
I started to run to it. I knew I had to get out.
That is when I heard something that made me stop...

Singin' Sally came groovin' down the stairs while she sang:
"Riley, do you think you need to run?..
If you do you'll miss all the fun... I have toys and a doggie treat...
Wiggle your fur and shake your feet."

Before I knew it, I was wagging my tail and dancing
with Singin' Sally. Lordy tried to dance with us, but he just
kept tripping over his big paws.

I was having so much fun that I didn't see Singin' Sally
walk out of the room. When I realized she was gone,
my heart began to race again.

I looked for her in the dining room... no Singin' Sally

So I stood very still. I perked up my ear and
listened closely. I was trying to hear
Singin' Sally's next song...

I even looked down
the hall...
no Singin' Sally

I peeked in the closet... no Singin' Sally

Suddenly, her voice sang out to me:
"Rockin' Riley keep moving your feet...
Come to the kitchen and get a treat."

When I made it to the kitchen, Singin' Sally rubbed my head
and smiled. She had walked to the kitchen to get me the
best toy ever - the Barkey Bone!
Any dog would love the Barkey Bone. It looks real,
but it squeaks... and it barks... and I can chew on it all day long.
Best of all, it has a secret spot in the middle for a special treat.

Singin' Sally put the Barkey Bone in my mouth and said,
"Come on Riley! Follow me!" We danced all the way up the stairs and
into the bathroom. She said the bathroom should be my "safe place"
during storms. How did she know that I'd feel safe in that big, empty
bathtub with all that banging & crashing going on during the storm?

I stayed in the bathtub chewing on my new toy for a long time. The special treat inside the Barkey Bone was peanut butter. By the time I gobbled it up, the storm was over. Whew!.. and I was safe!

So far, the Puppy Dog Power Plan worked. But that was just part of her plan. What else did she have in mind to teach me? Singin' Sally said the answer would come in the mail.

Two days later, the doorbell rang. The mailman handed Singin' Sally
a brown box. She then exclaimed, "The last part of the
Puppy Dog Power Plan is here!" She put the box on the table.
She said, "Riley, you are about to become a SUPERHERO!"

Singin' Sally opened the box and pulled out
the coolest thing I ever saw - a big, red cape with my name on it.
She calls it my Critter Cape, and it has a shiny silver lining.

Singin' Sally said there is something in the silver lining that keeps the flashes of lightning and the booms of thunder from making me feel so scared.

I wore my Critter Cape the whole first night,
which was lucky, because the meanest storm I ever saw
came charging through my neighborhood.

The sky lit up with a loud BOOM! The wind shook the house
and broke the branches of the trees. The rain slammed down
on the roof and poured over the gutters like a waterfall.
I jumped up. I looked out the window, and then...

I grabbed my Barkey Bone and danced my way to the bathroom.
I did this all on my own. I didn't even need to wake up Singin' Sally.
The Puppy Dog Power Plan rules!

Of course, I was still a little scared...
But I think I get it now. I understand that when I'm frightened,
I should play games and have a Bow-Wow Blast!
My Critter Cape will calm me down and give me courage.
I also know how to get to my "safe place."
But most of all, I know I have a mom who loves me.

I hope all the other dogs out there
have someone like Singin' Sally.
She helps me feel like a superhero
even when I don't wear my cape.

About the Author

Animal Gambill is a dedicated animal advocate

and children's book author. "Riley's Bow-Wow Blast" is the first

in an upcoming series of her children's books.

Animal Gambill is a Licensed Clinical Social Worker practicing as a child

therapist on a crisis unit for emotionally & behaviorally impaired children.

Her volunteer efforts for numerous animal welfare organizations include

everything from rescuing abandoned animals and fostering adoptable

pets to providing animal-assisted therapy, chairing fund-raisers,

and educating people about a variety of animal-related topics.

Animal Gambill's love for animals, combined with her appreciation for

the true spirit of children, inspired her to write a children's book series.

A portion of the proceeds from the book sales are donated

to various animal welfare organizations.

Mission Statement

Animal Gambill's Critter Crusade is a national tour whose mission is to educate and empower children and adults about a variety of animal welfare issues. The goal is to mutually enhance the quality of life of animals and their human companions. Through interactive educational efforts, the Critter Crusade will encourage children and adults to become an active, positive force in helping animals.

Animal Related Resources

Alley Cat Advocates, Inc ---*www.alleycatadvocates.org*

Alley Cat Allies ---*www.alleycatallies.org*

Animal Care Society ---*www.animalcaresociety.org*

Animal Protection Association ---*www.apa-pets.org*

ASPCA (American Society for the Prevention of Cruelty to Animals)
---*www.aspca.org*

Best Friends Animal Society ---*www.bestfriends.org*

Delta Society ---*www.deltasociety.org*

Doris Day Animal League ---*www.ddal.org*

Greyhounds of Shamrock---*www.greyhoundsofshamrock.org*

GRRAND (Golden Retriever Rescue and Adoption of Needy Dogs)
---*www.grrand.org*

Humane Society of the United States ---*www.hsus.org*

Pet Groups United ---*www.petgroupsunited.com*

Shamrock Foundation, Inc. ---*www.shamrockpets.com*

WAGS (Wonderful Animals Giving Support) ---*www.kywags.org*

The "Critter Cape" mentioned in "Riley's Bow-Wow Blast" is a therapeutic tool known as the **StormDefender Cape**. This cape was created by T.F. Critzer in order to reduce thunderstorm anxiety for dogs.
For more information, go to *www.StormDefender.com*